Dig Dig Digging

abc

For Alexi and Adela —M.M.
For Daisy and Blue —A.A.

Henry Holt and Company
Publishers since 1866
175 Fifth Avenue
New York, New York 10010
mackids.com

Henry Holt® is a registered trademark of Macmillan Publishing Group, LLC.
Text copyright © 2015 by Margaret Mayo
Illustrations copyright © 2015 by Alex Ayliffe
All rights reserved.
First published in the United States in 2017 by Henry Holt and Company
Originally published in England in 2015 by Orchard Books

Library of Congress Cataloging-in-Publication Data is available.
ISBN 978-1-62779-516-6

Our books may be purchased in bulk for promotional, educational, or business use. Please contact your local bookseller or the
Macmillan Corporate and Premium Sales Department at (800) 221-7945 ext. 5442 or by e-mail at MacmillanSpecialMarkets@macmillan.com.

Printed in China by Toppan Leefung Printing Ltd., Dongguan City, Guangdong Province
1 3 5 7 9 10 8 6 4 2

Dig Dig Digging

abc

Margaret Mayo

Alex Ayliffe

Henry Holt and Company
New York

Ambulance

Busy, busy ambulance
rush, rush, rushing.
whee-ow! whee-ow!
Loud siren blaring.

Bulldozer

Bb

Tough bulldozer
push, **push, pushing.**
Over bumpy ground,
scraping and shoving.

Cc

Crane

Very tall crane
lift,
lift,
lifting.
Up go the bricks
to the top of the building.

Digger

Dd

Great big digger
dig, **dig, digging.**
Scooping up the earth,
lifting and tipping.

Ee

Express Train

Super-fast express train
speed, speed, speeding.
Racing down the tracks—whoo-oom!
Passengers now boarding.

Ff

Fire Engine

Shiny red fire engine
dash, dash, **dashing.**

Nee-**nar!** Nee-**nar!**
Bright lights flashing.

Go-Karts

Sporty go-karts
race, **race, racing.**
Hurtling round the track,
dodging and chasing.

Hh

Helicopter

Bright yellow helicopter

whirr, whirr, whirring.

Hovering and swaying—

look!

Someone needs rescuing.

Icebreaker

Ii

Mighty icebreaker
crack, crack, cracking.
Plowing through the ice,
crunching and smashing.

Jj

Jumbo Jet

Enormous jumbo jet
roar, roar, roaring.
Over fields and buildings,
up . . . up . . .

Kk

Kayak

Racing river kayak
swoosh, swoosh, swooshing.
Rushing over rapids,
paddle safely guiding.

Long-Haul Truck

Hardworking long-haul truck
beep, **beep**, *beeping*.
Rumbling down the highway,
barely stops for sleeping.

Mm Motorbikes

High-speed motorbike

vroom, **vroom, vrooming.**

Jumping . . . swerving . . .

Watch that turn!

Daring, dirty riding!

Narrow Boat

Nn

Brightly painted narrow boat
chug, chug, chugging.
Along peaceful waterways,
slowly gliding.

Oo

Ocean Liner

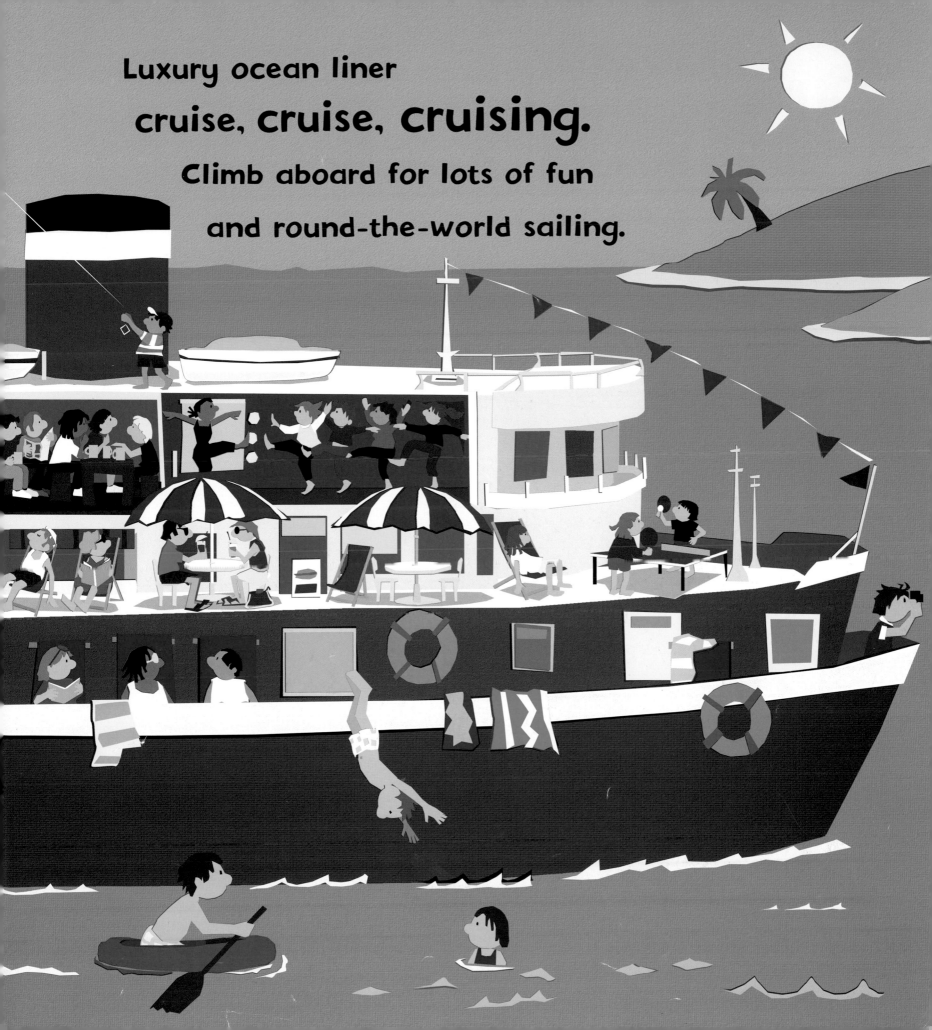

Luxury ocean liner
cruise, cruise, cruising.
Climb aboard for lots of fun
and round-the-world sailing.

Pp

Police Car

Emergency police car
scream,
scream,
screaming.
Slow down! Make way!
Police passing!

Qq

Quad Bike

Sturdy quad bike

bump, bump, bumping.

Along rough paths and up steep hills,

climbing and exploring.

Rr

Recycling Truck

Noisy recycling truck
gobble, **gobble**, **gobbling.**
Crunching, munching giant bags,
squeezing and squashing.

Ss

Scooter

Super little scooter
scoot, scoot, scooting.
Strong foot pushing,
and it's off . . . racing!

Tt

Tractor

Tough yellow tractor
pull, pull, pulling,
plowing up the field,
wheels squelch, squelching.

Underwater Robot

Uu

Roaming underwater robot dive, dive, diving.

In the deep, dark sea, lost-treasure hunting.

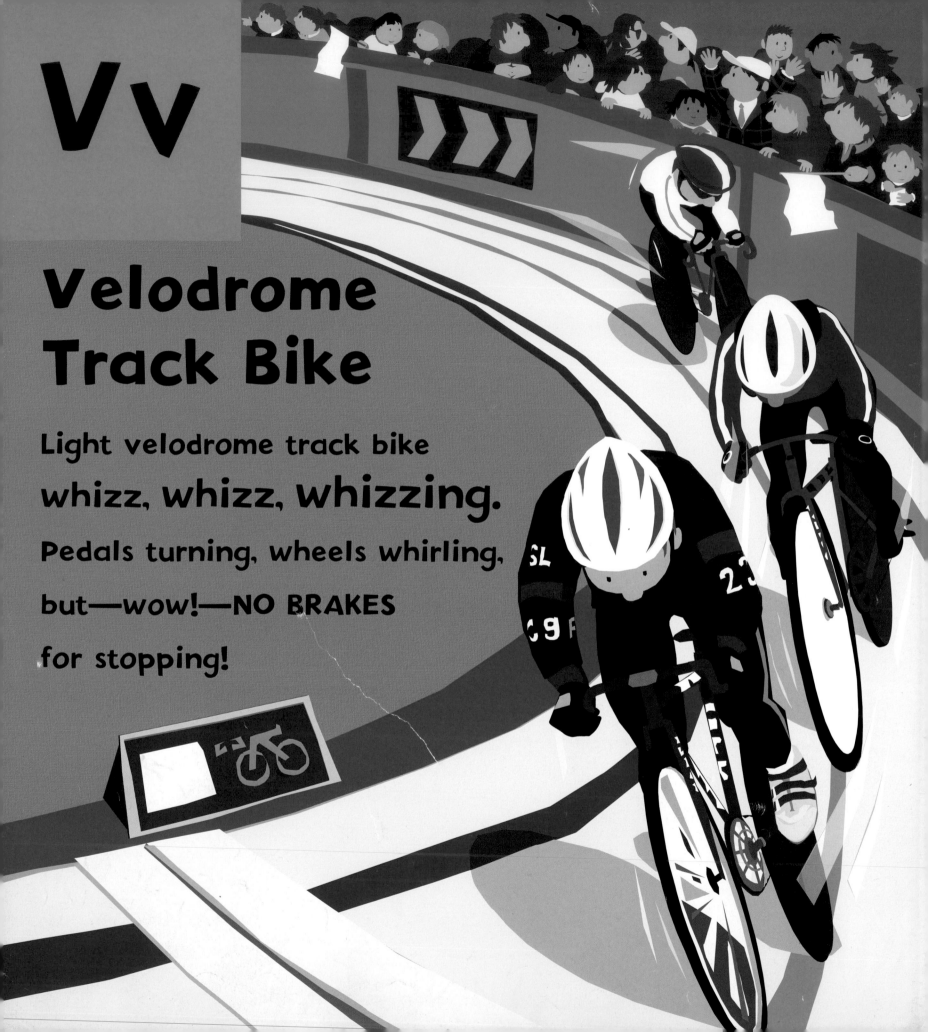

Vv

Velodrome Track Bike

Light velodrome track bike
whizz, whizz, whizzing.
Pedals turning, wheels whirling,
but—wow!—NO BRAKES
for stopping!

Ww

Windsurfing Board

Breezy windsurfing board swerve, **swerve**, **swerving**. Surfer holds on tight for fast water-riding!

Xx

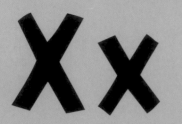

EXtra Big Wheels

EXtra-big-wheeled monster truck
grrhumm, grrhumm, grrhumming.
Fast racing, high jumping, and—
WHAM!—crazy wheel-standing.

Yacht

Beautiful yacht,
coast, **coast, coasting.**
Waves lapping, water splashing,
flag flap, flapping

Zz Zooming Rocket

Powerful rocket
zoom, zoom, **zooming.**
5 4 3 2 1 . . . and . . .
BLAST OFF!

outer-space
e**xploring!**